baby einstein®

WORDSWORTH's Book of Words

A Bilingual Book of Words

By Julie Aigner-Clark

Illustrations by Nadeem Zaidi

Hyperion Books for Children

The publisher wishes to thank the following for their permission to reprint the artwork in this book:

Chalkboard © C Squared Studios/Getty Images/PhotoDisc
Child by Mark Burr © Disney Enterprises, Inc.
Two babies/"And Baby Makes Three" © DigitalVision/PictureQuest
Girl holding an umbrella © C Squared Studios/PhotoDisc/PictureQuest
Toddler in sunglasses © Elyse Lewin/Brand X Pictures/PictureQuest
Girl in sundress © Elyse Lewin/Brand X Pictures/PictureQuest
Flip-flops © Ryan McVay/Getty Images/PhotoDisc
Girl raking autumn leaves © Russell Illig/Getty Images/PhotoDisc
Frame of children's shoes and socks © C Squared Studios/PhotoDisc/PictureQuest
Red mittens © C Squared Studios/PhotoDisc/PictureQuest
Child in snowsuit © Corbis Images/PictureQuest
Toy chest by Mark Burr © Disney Enterprises, Inc.
Beach ball © Joe Atlas/Brand X Pictures/PictureQuest
Soccer ball © Comstock IMAGES
Girl with doll carriage © Disney Enterprises, Inc.
Tricycle © C Squared Studios/PhotoDisc/PictureQuest
Boy on scooter © BananaStock/BananaStock, Ltd./PictureQuest
Doll © Stockpile/PictureQuest
Dollhouse © CMCD/PhotoDisc/PictureQuest
Baby Einstein puppet by Mark Burr © Disney Enterprises, Inc.
Rocking horse © Stockpile/PictureQuest
Teddy bear © Michael Lamotte/Cole Group/PhotoDisc/PictureQuest
Children in dress-up clothes © BananaStock/BananaStock, Ltd./PictureQuest
Blocks © Comstock IMAGES
Boy at easel © Comstock IMAGES
Crayons © Comstock IMAGES
Mother and child drawing © Comstock IMAGES
Water paint © Nancy R. Cohen/Getty Images/PhotoDisc
Paper dolls © EyeWire Collection/Getty Images
Doctor (1) © Comstock IMAGES
Girl with basketball © Comstock IMAGES
Family at birthday party © Bluestone Productions/SuperStock
Police officer and firefighter © David Hiller/PhotoDisc/PictureQuest
Doctor (2) © Comstock IMAGES
Nurse © Ryan McVay/PhotoDisc/PictureQuest
Ambulance driver © Comstock IMAGES
Soccer player © Comstock IMAGES
Ice-skater © EyeWire Collection/Getty Images
Hockey player © Comstock IMAGES
Scuba diver by Mark Burr/© Disney Enterprises, Inc.
Boy with basketball © RubberBall Productions/RubberBall Productions/PictureQuest
House © Amanda Clement/Getty Images/PhotoDisc
Child's bed © Corbis Images/PictureQuest
Crib © C Squared Studios/PhotoDisc/PictureQuest
Baby in pajamas © Corbis Images/PictureQuest
Night-light/"And Baby Makes Three" © DigitalVision/PictureQuest
Toddler in rocking chair © SW Productions/Getty Images/PhotoDisc
Mother and child reading © Image Source/Elektra Vision/PictureQuest
Refrigerator © C Squared Studios/PhotoDisc/PictureQuest
Stove © C Squared Studios/PhotoDisc/PictureQuest
Microwave © Stockpile/PictureQuest
Kitchen sink © C Squared Studios/PhotoDisc/PictureQuest
Kitchen table and chairs © Corbis Images/PictureQuest
High chair © Comstock IMAGES
Toilet © C Squared Studios/PhotoDisc/PictureQuest
Potty © C Squared Studios/PhotoDisc/PictureQuest
Towels © C Squared Studios/PhotoDisc/PictureQuest

Child brushing teeth © Elyse Lewin/Brand X Pictures/PictureQuest
Baby in bathtub © Elyse Lewin/Brand X Pictures/PictureQuest
Groceries © Comstock IMAGES
Child eating cereal © EyeWire Collection/Getty Images
Waffles © Comstock IMAGES
Pancakes © Comstock IMAGES
Yogurt container © EyeWire Collection/Getty Images
Banana © Comstock IMAGES
Hamburger © Comstock IMAGES
Boy eating pizza © SW Productions/Getty Images/PhotoDisc
Sandwich © Comstock IMAGES
Soup © Burke/Brand X Pictures/PictureQuest
Boy drinking milk © David Loc/SuperStock
Peanut butter on bread © Burke/Triolo/Brand X Pictures/PictureQuest
Chicken and broccoli © Michael Lamotte/Cole Group/PhotoDisc/PictureQuest
Taco © Comstock IMAGES
Rice © Burke/ Triolo/Brand X Pictures/PictureQuest
Salad © Comstock IMAGES
Birthday party © Stockbyte/PictureQuest
Noah's ark toy by Mark Burr © Disney Enterprises, Inc.
Child with puppies © Triolo/Brand X Pictures/PictureQuest
Goldfish © Triolo/Brand X Pictures/PictureQuest
Hamster © G. K. + Vicki Hart/PhotoDisc/PictureQuest
Hyacinth Macaw © Photo 24/Brand X Pictures/PictureQuest
Girl with kitten © SW Productions/Getty Images/PhotoDisc
Rabbit © G. K. + Vicki Hart/PhotoDisc/PictureQuest
Bear sow and cub © EyeWire Collection/Getty Images
Lioness © Comstock IMAGES
Zebra © Comstock IMAGES
Giraffe © Comstock IMAGES
African elephant © Jeremy Woodhouse/Getty Images/PhotoDisc
Monkey © Comstock IMAGES
Bald eagle © Alan and Sandy Carey/Getty Images/PhotoDisc
Bee © EyeWire Collection/Getty Images
Beetle © Lawrence Lawery/Getty Images/PhotoDisc
Wolf spider © Comstock IMAGES
Butterfly © Comstock IMAGES
Ladybug © Comstock IMAGES
Bottle-nosed dolphin © EyeWire Collection/Getty Images
Sea turtle © EyeWire Collection/Getty Images
Sweettips and squirrelfish © Michael Aw/Getty Images/PhotoDisc
Four masked butterflyfish © Georgette Douwma/Getty Images/PhotoDisc
Blue spotted stingray © Ian Cartwright/Getty Images/PhotoDisc
Gray reef shark © Ian Cartwright/Getty Images/PhotoDisc
Sea horse © DigitalVisition/PictureQuest
Crab © EyeWire Collection/Getty Images
Space shuttle © Stockbyte/PictureQuest
Bicycle © Comstock IMAGES
Bus © David Wasserman/Brand X Pictures/PictureQuest
Train © Comstock IMAGES
Wagon © Keith Brofsky/Brand X Pictures/PictureQuest
Mother pushing baby in stroller © C Squared Studios/Getty Images/PhotoDisc
Rowboat © Jack Hollingsworth/Getty Images/PhotoDisc
Sailboat © C. Lee/PhotoLink/PhotoDisc/PictureQuest
Airplane © Comstock IMAGES
Helicopter © Corbis Images/PictureQuest
Hot-air balloon © PhotoLink/Getty Images/PhotoDisc

Hyperion Books for Children, New York
Copyright © 2002 by The Baby Einstein Company, LLC.
All rights reserved.
Baby Einstein is a registered trademark of The Baby Einstein Company, LLC. All rights reserved.
Einstein and Albert Einstein are trademarks of The Hebrew University of Jerusalem. All rights reserved.
For information, address Hyperion Books for Children, 114 Fifth Avenue, New York, New York 10011-5690.
Printed in Singapore
ISBN: 0–7868–0883–7
Library of Congress Catalog Card Number: 2002104208
Cover and interior illustrations by Nadeem Zaidi

Visit www.hyperionchildrensbooks.com and www.babyeinstein.com

Me!

My Body

My Clothes

My Body

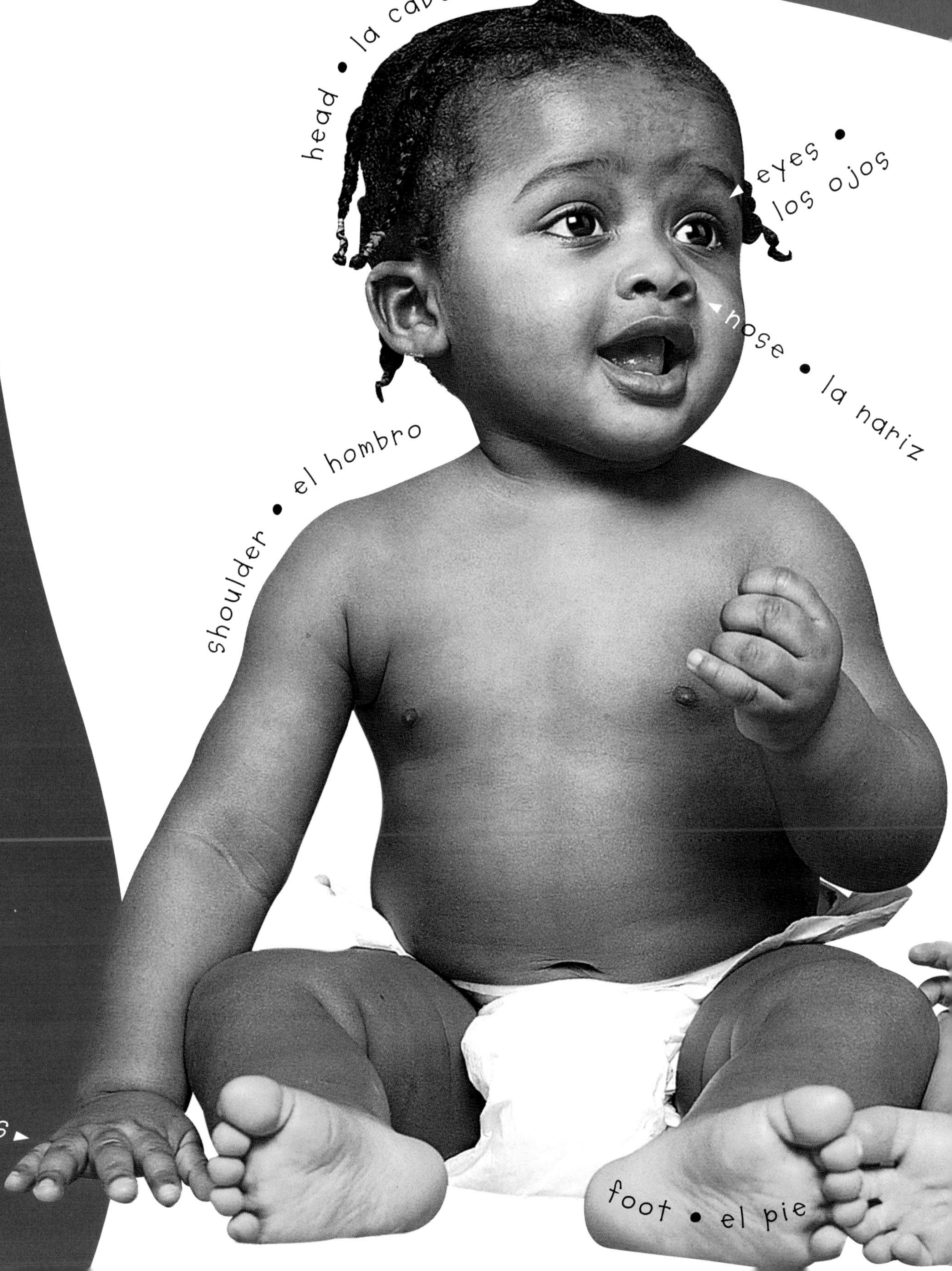

head • la cabeza

eyes • los ojos

nose • la nariz

shoulder • el hombro

fingers • los dedos

foot • el pie

What color is your hair?

Can you touch your nose? Your ears?

Draw a picture of yourself here. ▶

How many toes do you have?

hair • el cabello

ear • la oreja

mouth • la boca

arm • el brazo

tummy • el estómago ~~la pancita~~

hand • la mano

knee • la rodilla

los dedos del pie

toes

leg • la pierna

My Clothes

Me

socks • los calcetines

umbrella • el paraguas

sunglasses • las gafas de sol

raincoat • el impermeable

boots • las botas

Spring

sun hat • el sombrero para el sol

dress • el vestido

sandals • las sandalias

Summer

Why do people use umbrellas?

Can you find something shaped like a star?

Draw a silly hat here. ▶

What color are your favorite shoes?

autumn

◄ sweater •
el suéter

◄ pants •
el pantalón

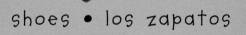

shoes • los zapatos

jacket • la chaqueta

winter

mittens • los mitones

hat • el gorro

scarf •
la bufanda ◄

snowsuit • el traje para la nieve

Me!

Paste or draw a picture of yourself in your favorite clothes here.

Toys

Roundup

Let's Pretend

Create

Roundup

soccer ball • la pelota de fútbol

doll carriage • el coche de muñecas

scooter • la patineta
el patinete

14

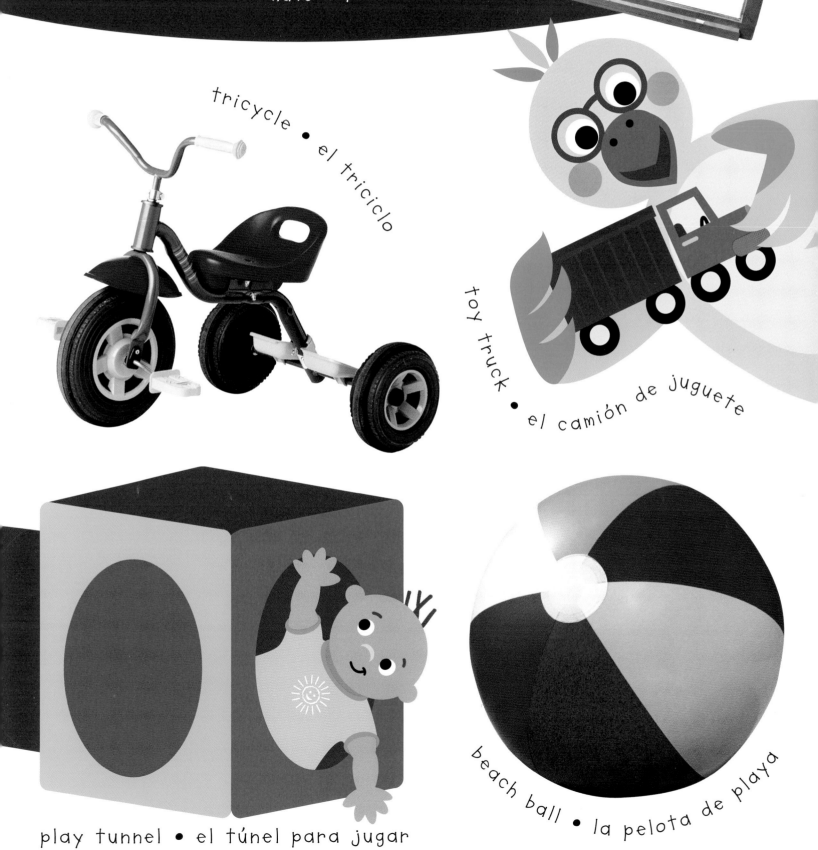

tricycle • el triciclo

toy truck • el camión de juguete

play tunnel • el túnel para jugar

beach ball • la pelota de playa

Let's Pretend

doll • la muñeca

dollhouse • la casa de muñecas

puppet • la marioneta

teddy bear • el osito

Point to the child dressed like a firefighter.

What dress-up clothes do you like to wear?

Draw a toy on the board. ▶

How many boxcars does the toy train have?

◀ toy train •
el trencito
el trencito

rocking horse • el caballito balancín

dress-up clothes • ponerse la ropa

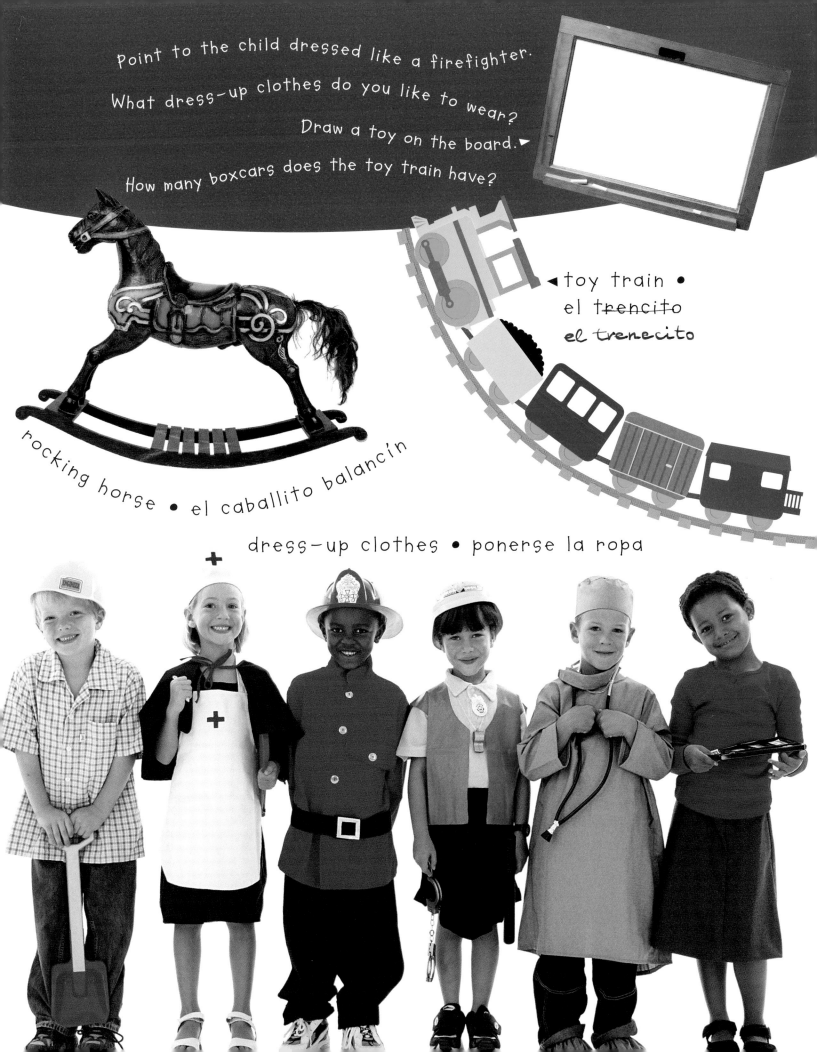

Create

water paint • la acuarela

crayons • los crayones

easel • el caballete

Can you name the letters on the toy blocks?

What is the boy at the easel painting?

Connect the dots to form a square. ▶

What color chalk is Wordsworth holding?

blocks • los bloques

chalk • la tiza

markers • los marcadores

paper dolls •
muñecas de papel

My Toys

Paste or draw a picture of your favorite toy here.

People

Family

Athletes

Community Helpers

People

grandfather • el abuelo

sister • la hermana

mother • la madre

What family members live with you?

Whose birthday is this family celebrating?
How can you tell?

Draw a birthday cake on the board. ▶

How old will you be on your next birthday?

father • el padre

brother • el hermano

grandmother • la abuela

baby • el bebé

Community Helpers

ambulance driver • el chófer de ambulancia

police officer • el policía

nurse •
la enfermera ▶

teacher • el maestro

How do police officers and firefighters help people?

What is your doctor's name?

Draw a fire truck here. ▶

Where do teachers work?

firefighter • el bombero

doctor • la doctora

bus driver • el chófer de autobús

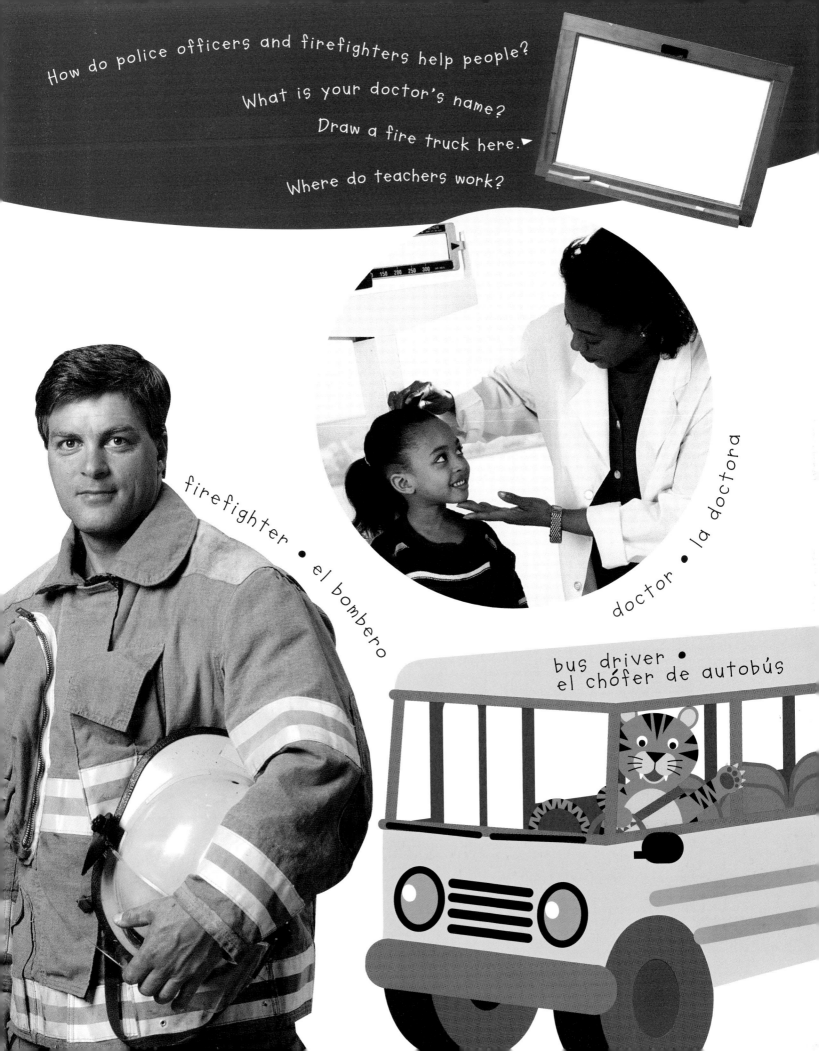

People

basketball player • el jugador de baloncesto básquetbol

horseback rider • el jinete

ice skater • la patinadora sobre hielo ▶

hiker • el excursionista

What two colors are on a soccer ball?

Why does a horseback rider wear a helmet?

Draw an orange basketball on the board. ▶

Which athletes wear ice skates?

hockey player •
el jugador de hockey

soccer player • el jugador de fútbol
o el futbolista

scuba diver • la buza
buceadora

My Family

Paste or draw a picture
of your family here.

House

Bedroom

Kitchen

Bathroom

Bedroom

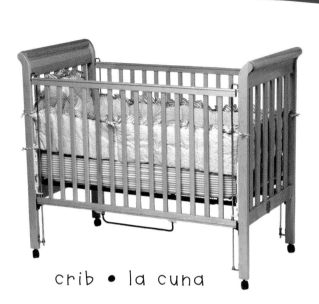

crib • la cuna

book • el libro

slippers • las zapatillas ~~pantuflas~~

pajama • el pijama

lamp • la lámpara

What kind of bed do you sleep in?

How many colors in the quilt can you name?

Connect the dots to draw a night star. ▶

What's your favorite bedtime story?

bed • la cama

night-light • la luz de noche

rocking chair • la mecedora

la colcha

quilt •

Kitchen

refrigerator • el refrigerador

la estufa

el horno

stove • la cocina

chair • la silla

Which appliances can make food hot?

Point to the appliance that keeps food cold.

Draw flowers to put in a vase for the table. ▶

Do you sit in a high chair or on a booster seat?

microwave oven •
el microondas

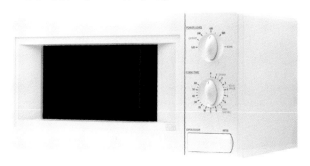

sink • ~~el lavaplatos~~
la fregadera

high chair • la silla alta para niños

table • la mesa

Bathroom

toilet • el inodoro
el váter

toothbrush • el cepillo de dientes

rubber duckie •
el patito de goma

bathtub • la tina

Do you like lots of bubbles in your bath?

What color is your toothbrush?

Draw a bath toy here. ▶

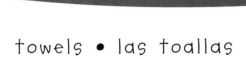

Who helps you wash your hair?

towels • las toallas

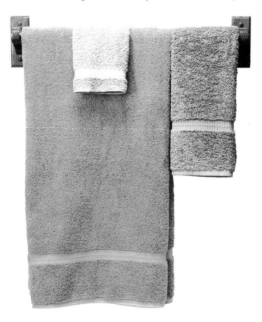

potty • la bacinica para niños

shower • la ducha

bubble bath • el baño de burbujas

My Room

Paste or draw a picture of your room here.

Food

Breakfast

Dinner

Lunch

Breakfast

yogurt • el yogur

cereal • el cereal

banana • el plátano

Point to a food that's round. Now find one that's square!

Which two foods could you eat with a spoon?

Write the letter P for "pancakes"! ▶

What's your favorite kind of juice?

waffles • los wafles

orange juice • **el zumo** • el jugo de naranja

pancakes • ~~los panqueques~~ las tortas

Food

milk • la leche

sandwich • el sándwich

jam • la mermelada

peanut butter • la mantequilla de maní cacahuate

Which two foods start with the letter S?

What's your favorite kind of sandwich?

Draw something that's the color of ketchup. ▶

Find a tomato on this page.

pizza • la pizza

soup • la sopa

hamburger • la hamburguesa

Dinner

broccoli • el brócoli

salad • la ensalada

taco • el taco

chicken • el pollo

Point to any food that is crunchy.

What wish do you think the birthday girl is making?

Draw a food that can go in a salad. ▶

How many yellow foods can you name?

rice • el arroz

birthday cake • la tarta de cumpleaños

corn on the cob • la mazorca de maíz

S

My Favorite Snack

Paste or draw a picture of your favorite snack here.

Animals

Pets

Bugs

Wild Animals

Ocean Animals

Pets

hamster • el hámster

goldfish • los peces dorados

puppy • el cachorro

Point to an animal you would like to have as a pet.

What would you name it?

Which animals have whiskers?

Connect the dots to form an animal. What is it? ▶

How many furry animals can you find here?

12
11
10
9
1
2
8
7
6
3
4
5

bunny • el conejo

parrot • el loro

kitten • el gatito

lizard • la lagartija

Wild Animals

bear • el oso

giraffe • la jirafa

lion • el león

zebras • las cebras

alligator • el caimán

48

Which animal has the longest neck? The biggest ears?

Point to an animal with spots. Which animal has stripes?

Write the first letter of the word *lion* here. ▶

How many monkeys do you see?

monkeys • los monos

eagle • el águila

elephant • el elefante

Bugs

beetle • el escarabajo

butterfly • la mariposa

ants • las hormigas

What bug names begin with the letter B?

How many legs does a spider have? A beetle?

Draw the black and yellow stripes of a bumblebee here. ▶

How is a butterfly like a dragonfly?

ladybug • la chinita o la mariquita

dragonfly • la libélula

spider • la araña

bee • la abeja

Ocean Animals

crab • el cangrejo

dolphin • el delfín

sea horse • el caballito de mar

sea turtle • la tortuga de mar

Point to two sea creatures with shells.

How is a shark like a dolphin? How is it different?

Draw a picture of a fish here. ▶

How do you think a sea horse got its name?

stingray • la mantarraya

tropical fish • los peces tropicales

whale • la ballena

shark • el tiburón

My Favorite Animal

Paste or draw a picture
of your favorite animal here.

Transportation

On the Ground

Air and Sea

On the Ground

train • el tren

stroller • el coche de bebés

school bus • autobús escolar

56

Which vehicle has only two wheels?

Which vehicle runs on tracks?

Connect the dots to see one more way to travel. ▶

How do *you* get from place to place?

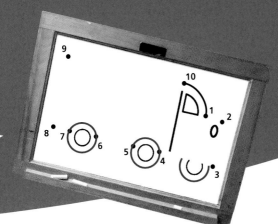

bicycle • la bicicleta

wagon • el carrito

car • el auto

Air and Sea

parachute • el paracaídas

sailboat • el velero

airplane • el avión

What shape is the sail on the sailboat?

In which vehicle would you like to ride?

Draw your own hot-air balloon here. ▶

How is an airplane like a bird?

helicopter • el helicóptero

hot-air balloon • globo aerostático

rowboat • el bote a remos

My Car Seat

Paste or draw a picture of yourself in your car seat here.

Ideas for Parents

A rich vocabulary, along with a multilingual awareness of language, enhances your child's relationship to the world. Language is, after all, a central means by which children learn about themselves and the people and things in their environment. Language also is a primary path toward self-expression. Here are some ways to make language-learning a part of your child's every day:

- **Introduce a variety of literary styles.** Storybooks, poetry, wordbooks, and even wordless books all present language in their own unique ways, helping children to expand vocabulary, focus on rhyme and imagery, and use imagination to provide their own narratives.

- **Play with words.** Children are enthralled by language in a number of ways—for its meanings and for its sounds. Use different words to describe the same object, such as *pail* and *bucket*. Helping your child to learn the multiple definitions of the objects and feelings they encounter every day develops playfulness and experimentation with language. Encourage your child to be alert to the sounds of words, too, by mimicking, for instance, sounds that are represented by words such as *splash* and *buzz*. On outings, search for words in the environment that your child encounters frequently, such as *stop* or *sale*.

- **Make word labels.** Help your child label his or her favorite possessions with words written on index cards. Write nouns or descriptive words, such as *houses*, *flowers*, or *yellow*, on large sheets of paper and encourage your child to cut out pictures that represent each word.